Anvil Press

Performance Series

MARK LEIREN-YOUNG'S

ARTICL*e*S *of* *f*AITH

THE BATTLE OF ST. ALBAN'S

A play about the blessing of same-sex relationships

Copyright © 2001 by Mark Leiren-Young

All rights reserved. No part of this book may be reproduced by any means without the prior written permission of the publisher, with the exception of brief passages in reviews. Any request for photocopying or other reprographic copying of any part of this book must be directed in writing to the Canadian Copyright Licensing Agency (CANCOPY) One Yonge Street, Suite 1900, Toronto, Ontario, Canada, M5E 1E5.

Printed and bound in Canada
Cover design: Webbervision
Author photo: Teresa Barbieri

Canadian Cataloguing in Publication Data

Leiren-Young, Mark 1962–
Articles of faith

ISBN 1-895636-41-8

I. Title
PS8573.E478A89 2001   C812'.54   C2001-910749-8
PR9199.3.L42A89 2001

Represented in Canada by the Literary Press Group
Distributed by General Distribution Services

The publisher gratefully acknowledges the financial assistance of the B.C. Arts Council, the Canada Council for the Arts, and the Book Publishing Industry Development Program (BPIDP) for their support of our publishing program.

Anvil Press Publishers
Suite 204-A 175 East Broadway
Vancouver, B.C. V5T 1W2
www.anvilpress.com

Contents

The Story of St. Alban's. v
Director's Notes ix
Cast of Characters. xi
Author's Notes. xii
Act I. 1
Act II 41

Acknowledgements

Thanks to my friends, family and especially my wife, Darron, for listening to me talk about Anglican Church politics for over a year. Thanks to Donna Wong-Juliani for refusing to let me say no to this, John Juliani and the original cast for bringing it to life, Joan Watterson for attempting to make sense of early drafts, Cindy Young and Diane Cheetham for setting me on the trail of St. Alban's and Don Atkins for his vision and making all of this possible. Thanks also to everyone who attended the two workshop productions especially, my parents, Hall and Carol Leiren and my brother David, for sharing their comments and concerns. Most importantly, I'd like to thank all the people I interviewed for their stories, their time, their trust and their candour.

The Story of St. Alban's

When I was approached to create a play dealing with the controversy surrounding the blessing of same sex unions in the Anglican Church, I immediately declined. I felt that regardless of what I wrote it would be dismissed by anybody who disagreed with any aspect of it as "biased" or "just the writer's imagination."

As a writer, I'm normally delighted to put both my imagination—and my biases—on stage. But the goal of the company commissioning me—Savage God—was to create a play that would spark a dialogue, and unless people on all sides of this issue were willing to watch the play, no dialogue was possible. Worse than being dismissed, I suspected that any play addressing this topic was likely to be ignored, since one of the biggest controversies for church congregations regarding the blessing of same sex unions is whether the issue should be discussed in the first place.

Then it hit me . . . the way to create characters people couldn't dismiss, or ignore, was to work entirely from real stories. I studied the work of Anna Deavere Smith, an American playwright specializing in docu-theatre, and decided to use her approach as a starting point.

After that, I put together an ambitious wish list of interview subjects and set out to assemble a play the way a government assembles a cabinet—with all types of representation. It sounded wonderful, in theory. As I started my research, I realized I had an issue but no story. The end result might be a fascinating collection of quotes but it was unlikely to work as theatre.

Then I came across the story of St. Alban's and, since it was a story nobody seemed to want to talk about, I knew it was worth investigating. The night after conducting my first interview I called the people who had commissioned me and told them two things: this was the story I wanted to tell, and it might not be a story they wanted to hear.

I had found a congregation that, for all intents and purposes, excommunicated themselves from the Anglican community because they felt it was becoming too liberal. There were other reasons that 120 out of 135 people voted to "disaffiliate" from the Anglican church—ranging from theological disputes to disagreements over the allocation of church funds—but everybody I spoke to confirmed that the issue of same sex unions was a catalyzing one.

Once I'd found the story, it was simply a matter of finding the voices to tell it. I set out to write a script choosing snapshots from various conversations to capture the story and, hopefully, the emotion behind what happened at St. Alban's.

The "Vancouver Island Priest" wasn't directly involved in the St. Alban's story, but crossed paths, and theological swords, with the pastor who ran the parish. I felt his voice was vital to the play and opened several doors to other stories and points of view.

Although only one person I spoke with requested anonymity, after careful consideration, and lengthy consultations with the director, we decided not to directly identify any of the people interviewed. We felt that the play spoke louder—and hopefully more universally—with characters being identified through their relationship to the church, as opposed to by name. Another extremely important reason for this approach was that the only name from St. Alban's that actually appeared in the body of any of the quotes I wanted to use was that of the former pastor.

I felt that by using his name—but no one else's—the play not only seemed unbalanced but reinforced the idea that what happened with St. Alban's was all about one man. And my research clearly indicated that this was not the case.

As a result, rather than alter the shape or context of a quote I created a pseudonym. I also changed the name of one person quoted in the *Diocesan Post*. These pseudonyms are the only changes in wording. However, in some cases I have avoided mentioning people's accents, or other characteristics of their speech, in order to preserve some degree of anonymity.

With every quote in the script, I've not only attempted to transcribe the words but also made every effort to convey the pauses, mood and inflections. I hope that I've also captured the concern, the humour and the passion.

MARK LEIREN-YOUNG
TORONTO, MAY, 2001

Director's Notes

When I was approached by a parishioner about the feasibility of creating a play that might allow those with widely divergent views on the subject of the blessing of same-sex relationships to see themselves reflected, as it were, on the stage, and by so doing help exorcise whatever struggles were "possessing" them, the temptation was impossible to resist.

Articles of Faith: The Battle of Saint Alban's was commissioned in the Fall of 1999 with the generous help and impetus of a concerned Anglican parishioner who was anxious to help defuse what seemed to be shaping up as a highly contentious and politically explosive issue. The collaboration with Mark Leiren-Young seemed natural and inevitable. On two previous occasions (*Dim Sum Diaries*—1991; *Shylock*—1996) Savage God and the playwright had grappled with controversial and socially relevant subjects, and this assignment promised to be equally challenging. Once the documentary approach had been decided upon, and the research and interviewing done, all that remained was to convey to an audience, in a virtually verbatim fashion, what a representative cross-section of the people of one parish had to say about their momentous decision to leave the Anglican church.

A word of warning. As theatre practitioners we have our biases and convictions and preconceptions, like anyone in the audience or anyone who may be reading this playscript. We do not claim any particular expertise on the issue that is at the centre of *Articles of Faith*, nor do we feel it is our "job" to change anyone's mind. We do not allow ourselves the luxury of proselytizing. We see our task as simple and straightforward: to present as clearly as possible, with a minimum of theatricality, the words, thoughts, and insofar as we can, the feelings, of specific, actual individuals for whom the issues articulated in this play were burning issues, issues that changed the course of their lives.

No one, even if they have minimal knowledge of what happened at St. Alban's, could imagine that the process of rupture was a painless one. Is change ever achieved without a modicum of pain? But also painful and equally instructive is the inevitable, deep-seated and completely understandable resistance to change, in which most of us sheathe ourselves in our day to day existence.

I believe that if Theatre is to be the transformative experience that it can be, it is essential that those of us who engage in it—actors and audience members alike—actively entertain the notion that preconceptions, however set, and convictions, however sharply held, are subject to alteration. The process of self-awareness and reconciliation that can come out of a frank dialogue about fundamental and often unspoken views requires, at the very least, an open mind and an open heart.

It is in that context that *Articles of Faith: The Battle of Saint Alban's* was commissioned, conceived, and created; and it is in the spirit of generosity, respect, and a genuine hope of better understanding that we share it with you.

JOHN JULIANI
Founder & Artistic Director
Savage God

Time: The parishioners at St. Alban's "disaffiliated" in 1996. The interviews took place in the year 2000.

Articles of Faith premiered at Christ Church Cathedral in Vancouver, Canada on May 30, 2001, under the direction of John Juliani, with the following cast:

JOHN JULIANI
Reporter/Narrator

MARILYN NORRY
Female Parishioner #1
Female Parishioner #2
Wife

ALLAN MORGAN
Former Youth Pastor
Husband
Catholic Priest
Rev. Fred Phelps

WILLIAM SAMPLES
Former Pastor of St. Alban's (David)
Father Bill Bacon

ROBERT MOLONEY
Vancouver Island Priest
The New Rector of St. Alban's

Author's Notes

The length of beats, pauses and sighs is generally a directing or acting decision, but the goal with this script was to attempt to capture the reality of these conversations and, as a result, the pauses taken by the interview subjects were actually timed. The "beats" here are two seconds long. The "pauses" are three seconds long.

Although "rector" is the traditional term for Anglican parish leaders, "pastor" was the term preferred by both the former leader of St. Alban's and the former youth leader and have been used accordingly.

Casting

The premiere production featured five actors. However, the size of the cast can range depending on the number of performers available. In addition to casting one actor in each role, you can increase community involvement by casting multiple performers in the role of "Reporter." The hope is that this script will be produced in a wide variety of communities, and my suggestion is to use as large a cast as possible and, if possible, to cast people in roles contrary to their personal beliefs.

Rights to produce *Articles of Faith*, in whole or in part, in any medium by any group, amateur or professional, are retained by the author. Interested persons are requested to apply to: Playwrights Union of Canada, 54 Wolseley St., 2nd Floor, Toronto, Ontario M5T 1A5, tel: (416) 703 0201 fax: (416) 703 0059 info@puc.ca

ACT I

Our cast is singing a hymn. It should be beautiful and set a tone of spirituality and worship. The style of the music is modern and infectious. The Reporter *takes focus—he/she is holding a newspaper.*

REPORTER: *Diocesan Post* February, 1996.

Stating that they were, "profoundly troubled by the compromising position that the Anglican church has taken in key areas of the Christian faith," members of the congregation of St. Alban's, Port Alberni, voted overwhelmingly to quit the Anglican church. They have decided to form a new, non-denominational community church with a form of worship resembling the traditional Anglican church liturgy. The vote on "disaffiliation" from the Anglican church was approved by 120 of the 135 people who attended what was described as, "a lengthy and emotional meeting," that was open only to members of the congregation.

Female Parishioner #1: *Maternal, compassionate and genuine. Early 40s. The interview took place at a table in a small town Chinese restaurant. She drank tea while we spoke. Her husband sat beside her, speaking occasionally. The husband can be beside her here. Or not.*

FEMALE PARISHIONER #1: They had so many people coming to church that people couldn't go up and kneel at the altar. It just was taking too long.

The service wasn't over till 2 o'clock in the afternoon. And you're starting at ten. We would have to go at nine o'clock to get a seat. People were on benches, they were on chairs. It was so full . . .

Our Sunday school was so full we were using the priest's office for Sunday school.

It was just filled with people.

She fades back into the service, singing with the others.

REPORTER: British Columbia. *Diocesan Post.* March, 1996. "Port Alberni Parish Tries to Return to Normal"

Bishop Warden Matthew Curtis says there's only one word to describe the break-up at St. Alban's church here—"devastating."

He says it's something akin to divorce which can create wounds that will take a long time to heal.

"All we can do now is try to make a go of it, but it won't be easy."

FEMALE PARISHIONER #1: When we were there the Church was feeding the poor. They were running a store that was feeding the poor. Developing programs—

There's a high rate of illiteracy in Port Alberni. And so they were developing programs to teach people how to read and write. And so the Church was stopping from being that "nice place." Our beautiful church hall was filled with freezers of food and we were feeding people.

For example, every year the church would have this wonderful Christmas bazaar. Well, the money, instead of going into the church coffers, was being sent out to places like Camp Columbia, out to feed people, to do things other than buy something for the congregation.

REPORTER: Disgruntled former members of the parish, led by Rector David Adams, have rented a hall in the local Christian school and formed the Alberni Christian Fellowship . . .

The hymn continues and the focus shifts to The Former Youth Pastor *at St. Alban's. He left with the rest of the congregation to help found the Alberni Christian Fellowship. He's now 37. This interview took place over the phone. He was in his office at his new job in Colorado. He sounds young and enthusiastic—like someone used to working with teens.*

YOUTH PASTOR: It eases the minds and the emotions of most of the people in the Anglican church to think— oh it was just some rogue guy. It was some . . .
you know . . .

(pause)

Jimmy Jones kind of charismatic guy who led these people astray. And that really isn't the feeling of the general masses. They don't like to see that no, it was the everyday common Joe.

David, the Pastor: *He's articulate, passionate and determined to tell his story properly. Early-40s. He seems a bit weary—like someone telling war stories he has no interest in reliving—but he also seems a bit relieved to be talking to someone who is actually listening. The interview took place in a small, corporate-style office. He sat at his desk, occasionally getting up to walk or pace.*

DAVID: I see a church that's lost its core. It's lost its heart, it's lost its way. And I think the homosexual issue . . .

It's like apartheid in South Africa . . .

It crystallized things. You basically then had to respond to that in some way. And then your response will tell you something about who you are and who we are and everything else.

So the homosexuality issue forces the debate about a theology, debate about authority, debate about identity.

Female Parishioner #2: *A confident, articulate professional in her 30s. The interview was at the kitchen table. We ate soup while we spoke.*

FEMALE PARISHIONER #2: I guess too the question is, and part of this is what people struggle with, is what is the line? What is the line that pushes people to say I no longer want to be a part of the church? And is this an issue which does symbolize—is this a good issue to hang one's hat on, okay? And that's probably going to end up being different for different people. But there are many other individuals and churches who probably think a lot like we did but they haven't got to their point yet of saying, I have to separate. But they've got their line drawn as when the church does accept same sex marriage, or whatever, well then we'll leave.

Or they've got maybe different things or different timelines for what they would then do. And I think there are other people out there and I guess . . . I guess what is different about that is we didn't wait for the line in the sand to be crossed, it was kind of more like just a growing . . .

To kind of grow away from something and saying this doesn't fit anymore.

ARTICLES OF FAITH

REPORTER: Human Sexuality: A Statement by the Anglican Bishops of Canada—1997.

Blessing of Covenanted Relationships:

We continue to believe that committed same sex relationships should not be confused with Holy Matrimony. The house will not authorize any act that appears to promote this confusion.

There is, and needs to be, ongoing discussion about how to respond appropriately to faithful and committed same sex relationships. In the context of the ongoing debate, this would necessitate respectful listening and learning about the nature of such relationships and their meaning for the persons involved in them.

We recognize that relationships of mutual support, help and comfort between homosexual persons exist and are to be preferred to relationships that are anonymous and transient.

We disagree among ourselves whether such relationships can be expressions of God's will and purpose.

Husband and Wife: *A couple in their 60s. They're beyond comfortable with each other and their conversation flows like they've been married forever. They finish each other's sentences without missing a beat. A kitchen table interview . . . We drank tea.*

WIFE: Everything I read in scripture is not conducive to being a homosexual.

But at the same time it's not for us to condemn that person and that's not to say that we would not accept that person into fellowship. Yes, we would. But there comes a point where you have to be responsible when you take leadership on.
                (*her tone softens*)

Now we know that this is flying in the face of human rights these days. We know that somewhere along the line I'm sure that this is all going to come up in the human rights aspect because um, and this is where living by the scriptures is gonna be tough.

HUSBAND: I think there's a stronghold of gays and so forth in the Anglican headquarters in Toronto, which is the centre for all Anglican propaganda that they send out.

So you've got a strong support of the gay movement, the homosexual movement, built into the hierarchy of the Anglican church in Toronto, so naturally they're going to push in all their information and stuff that this is—

WIFE: They have a strong lobby—

HUSBAND: Same as the feminists, they want to change the name of God to Mother God or—

WIFE: Sofia—

HUSBAND: Doesn't have to be a male.

WIFE: The goddess of wisdom.

DAVID: I think that the issue of homosexuality crystallizes, within the Anglican church, its . . .
> *(pause)*

Its propensity to . . .
> *(two beats)*

It values diversity almost above everything. And its ability to hold in tension diverse opinions. The problem with that is that it doesn't test or debate its diverse opinions very much—it merely presumes that everybody accepts diversity without qualification. And that's fine until you come to a place where you have to say—is there anything that is a core value for this church that is nonnegotiable to those who come to be members of it? The issue that homosexuality brought up for me was, what is the authoritative centre of this church? Is there any? Where we can make an appeal saying our core values say we can't go here or go there. Are there any nonnegotiables? Is there anything about the Christian faith that we think is so fundamental that we submit to it or we say maybe this is not for me?
> *(beat)*

So the homosexual issue for me crystallized the question of identity and the question of biblical authority.
> *(pause)*

The problem in the discussion in the Anglican church in my experience is that everything gets caricatured very quickly and very easily. So instead of answering questions that are legitimately raised, they're pushed aside or processed ad nauseam. So it becomes a moving target that never gets defined.

Vancouver Island Priest: *A sturdy, confident man in his 40s, wearing a clerical collar under a nice sweater. An interview in a church office on Vancouver Island.*

VANCOUVER ISLAND PRIEST: God is pure being . . .

But all of us creatures are not pure being and we can't separate our meaning from our action.

That is where it becomes such a difficulty because they'll say okay . . . only . . .

The only context in which sexual intimacy between two people is allowable is marriage. Marriage is only allowed between a man and a woman. So only heterosexual couples—in marriage—can have intimate sexual relationships . . . No one else can . . . And that simply means, of course, because marriage is by definition heterosexual, that gay couples—no matter how monogamous, no matter how committed, no matter how deeply loving they are, their intimate relationships are always sinful. And unredeemable.

It's a wonderfully consistent argument . . . It just happens to destroy people's lives.
(double pause)

And say that that's okay because they're sinners.
(two beats)

And it also ends up—you end up with a lot of people who marry in the conventional sense, hoping that marriage will either cure them or they'll be able to get along okay or whatever. But they end up living a lie. And nothing more damaging can happen—

I've known a couple of women that this has happened to where their husbands left them for other men—and all of the sudden they realize, everything we had together was a lie.

(his voice softens)

And it's utterly destructive.

DAVID: The homosexual debate looked and felt like it was an erosion that was just a matter of time. In other words, it's a bit like the Quebec thing, let's have another referendum until we get "yes." That's what I figure the homosexual issue is in the Anglican church—that basically it'll go on and on and on until it's legitimized. And it really doesn't matter how long it takes.

And what I saw is the liberal wing very willing to do that. And a conservative wing, very naive. And saying, well we must keep on talking. And I think, of course you keep on talking but there's a point where you say no—we cannot reconcile these two differences. And I think the problem in the Anglican church is dealing with the fact they have two irreconcilable differences in theologies that will never meet.

(two beats)

And it's enormously time-consuming, it's enormously emotionally draining and I think it's enormously futile in the end. You know, because you're saying what is the purpose of the church? Is it to spend all our time grappling and navel-gazing and wondering about ourselves, or is it to do something a little bit more than this?

So it's an important issue, but I think it became just a too all-consuming issue. So that issue, and the ongoing reality of that issue—underneath that issue was the issue of the authority of scripture. Where does scripture stand, where is scripture? And we can spend all afternoon talking about that—in terms of an authority base for the Anglican church. And I don't think it has one anymore. I don't think it counts. It's part of—but it's like a very floating . . .

so if you take that away no matter . . .
(sigh)

I'm not one who goes by an absolute conservative fundamentalist interpretation of scripture . . .

But it seems to me you have to have something to aim for. You have to have something around which to build an identity. And I think that there are enough core issues that you can agree on to say these things, these few things are nonnegotiable. Beyond that there are lots of interpretations that we'll spend the rest of our lives working out.

An email from a former Anglican priest who converted to Catholicism and became a Catholic priest due to his theological disagreements with the Anglican Church.

CATHOLIC PRIEST: Dear Mark: After some further consideration, I regret that my conscience will not permit me to participate in your project.

Please do not take this as a personal rejection. Part of my Anglican, and now Catholic 'position,' is that by participating in a debate on homosexuality, which a faction of the church has introduced, I tacitly legitimize the position that the expression of homosexual intimacy is a Christian option.

After much prayer and thought, I have concluded that to pull out of the 'dialogue,' and simply get on with the job of proclaiming the gospel, is the most faithful course of action.

Sorry to disappoint you.

VANCOUVER ISLAND PRIEST: At the same time those who preach . . .what I would consider to be . . . anti-homosexual . . .slant are very quick to distance themselves from those who translate the content of that preaching into action. And bash people or whatever . . .

I got into trouble at the Diocesan Synod here a couple of years ago just after the Matthew Shepard incident where we had a debate on . . . some aspect of the homosexual question. And I don't remember just what it was but I said . . .

I stood up and said I want to put a human face on this discussion and read comments that I had got on the internet from the priest who had been ministering to Matthew and his family in the hospital. And people thought I was being . . .

I was throwing in a red herring, trying to distract us and that wasn't what they were talking about at all. They wouldn't allow that there was any continuity between the kind of anti-gay rhetoric that was being spoken in the synod and that kind of anti-gay action. Now . . . I myself think there is a continuity . . .
(two beats)

Because if you give people permission to hate, then they're going to express that hatred.

A sermon from Father Bill Bacon, *St. Paul's Episcopal Church, Ft. Collins, Colorado. This was forwarded by email to The Vancouver Island Priest and many other Anglicans.*

BILL BACON: The phone rang on a Saturday afternoon as I was finishing the Sunday sermon.

Would I come to the hospital and meet with the family of Matthew Shepard and would I come prepared to administer Last Rites? Matthew is the 21-year-old man beaten, robbed and left for dead, hanging like a scarecrow on a fence outside Laramie, Wyoming.

As we were gathered in a side room, waiting for nurses to complete some medical procedures, Judy, Matthew's mother, told me how her son loved the Episcopal church. He chose to be confirmed at age 15, served as an acolyte in his parish in Casper, Wyoming. Attended Canterbury Club while at the University of Wyoming. He had recently attended a service at an Episcopal church in Denver and had felt rejected for being gay. Yet he had expressed determination to remain in the church he loved. Matthew was known as a kind, gentle person, who took everybody at face value, and did not see the bad side to anyone.

Gathered around his bandaged body, we began the Litany at the Time of Death.

As lights blinked and the respirator purred, I thought of the obscenity of the Lambeth Resolution on Sexuality. Especially the bit included as an afterthought, and not unanimously: "We wish to assure them—homosexuals—that they are loved by God and that all baptized, believing and faithful persons, regardless of sexual orientation, are full members of the Body of Christ." Matthew, a child of God by baptism . . .

A Son of the Episcopal church.

The obscenity of even thinking that a vote had to be taken to ensure that he was a full member of the church.

Jesus, Lamb of God: have mercy on us.

The respirator continued to purr as I anointed his sacred head with oil.

Our diocesan convention. The obscenity of even having the thought of considering the Lambeth Resolution on Sexuality as diocesan policy. What are we, what are we considering becoming?

Jesus, bearer of our sins, have mercy on us.

Pray for our Bishops, and for Jerry, our Bishop. That he may have clarity of thought, courage, and a strong heart. Pray for each other, that we may listen and that we may remember what a precious gift the Episcopal church is to us. The Faith is a constant, the Episcopal church is not. We can destroy it with our agendas. Pray for ourselves that we may put aside hysteria over human sexuality.

Matthew Shepard is a treasure to the Church, as we each are treasures. Gay and Lesbian men and women serve at God's altars, celebrate Eucharist for us, serve on our vestries and sit in our pews. We don't have to vote on their membership; they are full members and the time has come to work together for the things that need to be done for God's Kingdom.

Matthew entered into Paradise on October 12. God did not ask him his sexual orientation. God asked him if he loved his Lord and did he love his fellow humans and seek to serve them, and did he try to find a bit of Christ in those he met.

Let us pray that we can answer as well as Matthew when our time comes.

Jesus, redeemer, redeemer of the world; give us your peace.

Give us your peace.

VANCOUVER ISLAND PRIEST: Fred Phelps is the guy from Westward Baptist Church in Kansas City or whereever it is, reads the Bible and is able to take what he sees of the Bible and translate that into banners that say, "God hates fags."

And to praise AIDS as God's way to get rid of the fags.

And to go to AIDS funerals and praise God for killing another one. That's the kind of thing he does. He got a lot more coverage with Matthew Shepard than he has with others.

But that's the kind of thing he does . . .

But he's reading that out of the Bible.

From the Western Baptist Church website: "Matthew Shepard's Message From Hell" at godhatesfags.com.

Date: today.

(Please update the number of days in hell before each performance to replace the number "542." Shepard died: Oct. 12, 1998.)

Phelps has a Southern US accent and an evangelical style of preaching.

FRED PHELPS: Matthew Shepard has been in hell for 542 days.

Eternity minus 542 days equals Eternity.

When Matthew Shepard died on October 12, 1998, every pervert in this country—from Bill Clinton on down—used his death as a soapbox to promote so-called "gay rights."

In religious protest of this, Western Baptist Church picketed the funeral of Matthew Shepard, to inject a little truth and sanity into the irrational orgy of lies consuming this world.

WBC does not support the murder of Matthew Shepard, and we believe that his murderers are in violation of God's commandment that "thou shalt not kill." Unless they repent, they will receive the same sentence that Matthew Shepard received—eternal fire.

However, the truth about Matthew Shepard needs to be known. He lived a satanic lifestyle. He got himself killed trolling for anonymous homosexual sex in a bar at midnight.

Unless he repented in the final hours of his life, he is in hell. He will be in hell for all eternity, "*where their worm dieth not, and the fire is not quenched.*" Mark 9:44. For each day that passes, he has only eternity to look forward to.

All the candlelight vigils, all the tributes, all the acts of congress, all the rulings by the Supreme Court of the United States, will not shorten his sentence by so much as one day. And all the riches of the world will not buy him one drop of water to cool his tongue.

"Thou shalt not lie with mankind, as with womankind: it is abomination." Leviticus 18:22.

FEMALE PARISHIONER #1: God doesn't hate homosexuals. Anybody who tells you that doesn't—

has not got much of a relationship with God. He never says that he hates homosexuals. He doesn't like the practice of it. So you know, and I think, and Christ, Christ loves people and we're taught to love. And no matter what I say or what I do, if I don't act in love, Paul says I'm a clanging gong. So how can I look at you . . .

(her soft voice gets even softer)

Who my Lord and Saviour died for—and not listen to what you have to say, not treat you with respect and not value you above myself. I can't. I can't and say to Jesus, "I love you Lord."

(beat)

You're precious—

(pause)

And I can't, I can't look at anybody. I don't judge people. That's not my place. It's not my place to judge you. I am called to love you, to serve you, to be your sister. And if you're practicing or doing something that's bad, I'm going to love you and serve you and be your sister.

(beat)

It's the Holy Spirit that'll speak to your spirit and change you. I'm never gonna condemn you. And I think that we in the church so often reserve the right to judge. And I don't think we have that right.

(two beats)

The only right that I have is to love. And that means laying down my life and saying to the Lord, yeah, okay, how do I bring you to Light today. But the Bible is pretty solid in its teaching . . .

We so often take the Bible and use it against one another. And that isn't what God meant the word of God for and there's nowhere anywhere in the New Testament where Jesus ever says, "I hate you." His command was to love one another, not judge one another.

(beat)

That was the teaching I've learned in the Anglican church and from the Priests I was in contact with.

VANCOUVER ISLAND PRIEST: The church is able to handle gays if it involves them one at a time. But if they come in pairs then they have a problem.

(laughs)

Because, officially, we can cope with them as individuals whether we think of them as visible sinners, or eccentrics or whatever. And we can even kind of sort of overlook the fact that they actually live in a house with somebody else of the same sex and even share the same bed. But when they come to us and ask us . . . "please, bless this relationship of ours," then we have to say oh no no no no. He can come, and you can come, but you can't come together.

(laughs)

DAVID: There's no question I'm cynical. For the last fifteen years it's been, let's talk and listen. And that's why I say it feels like this French Quebec thing . . .

Which I've said before. You want me to listen until I eventually say yes. And I go, "can't you hear no?" Is that not legitimate?

Can you respect my "no" and stop asking me to say yes . . .

And not call me names and not tell me that I'm this and that and the other thing. I'm not doing that to you . . .

I'm not standing up insulting you for being homosexual. I'm not calling you names. I'm not chastising you . . .

But if I stand up and say I disagree, you call me names, you insult me, you attack me personally, you get hysterical . . .

It just doesn't seem like a balanced field to me.

Where's the justice in this and the acceptance and the love and the caring and all this stuff . . .

And that's why I'm cynical, because I don't think it's a level field. I think there's a very strong lobby group that will stop at nothing other than its own legitimacy. And to my mind the only way to deal with a strong minority lobby group is to be equally strong and say no . . . that way is not gonna work.

I don't know . . . I don't know. I think there are irreconcilable differences . . .

And I think the roots of those irreconcilable differences have been the Anglican church's lack of clarity over its core issues over the last forty or fifty years.

Maybe even longer.

WIFE: This wasn't done over a year or two, you know. This was over a ten-year period of bit by bit by bit. Just finding that we were . . .
> *(beat)*

not in the same realm as our . . .
> *(beat)*

so-called leaders.

HUSBAND: The best description of what the Anglican church is doing is . . . You've heard the story about putting a pot of water on the stove with cold water and putting a frog in it. And turning the heat on. He'll stay in there until he dies. Because it's a gradual change, gradual change. And if you put a frog into hot water he'll jump out.

But with a gradual build up and change—and this is what the Anglican church has done—they gradually have eroded the principles of the Christian faith so subtly that half of the people don't realize it's happening until it's too late. Same as the frog. He dies because he hasn't moved out of that and the water's getting too hot.

So this is exactly what they do. And they take little by little—it's the feminists, then it's the homosexual, then it's the hymn books. Then you've got to take out *Onward Christian Soldiers*. I mean, a traditional hymn because it's got—

WIFE: Because it was too militant.

HUSBAND: It's too—

WIFE: *(starts to laugh)*

HUSBAND: And everybody knows *Onward Christian Soldiers*. But they wouldn't allow that in the new hymn book. It's stuff like that, that eventually you say aaaaah . . . I can't take anymore of this.

WIFE: *(stops laughing)* It's . . . It's a sad state I think of— affairs. And I believe the Anglican church is going to shoot itself in the foot so badly that it's going to die. It is dying.

HUSBAND: Yeah.

WIFE: The only Anglican churches that are still growing are the ones that are trying to keep to—they're trying to ignore—what is being pushed on them.

DAVID: The thing I found most offensive in the issue about the discussion of homosexuality . . .

was the inability to disagree . . .

without being labeled homophobic. I do not regard myself as fundamentalist, conservative, homophobic. But the caricature is that.

FEMALE PARISHIONER #1: The only teaching that I ever remember getting from St. Alban's—and it came from every priest that had ever been in there in the time I was there—that homosexuality . . . a homosexual could be a Christian, could be a practicing Christian, but you couldn't be practicing homosexuality.

And that if you were there, if you were unmarried, you were celibate—whether you were heterosexual or homosexual. And that's the only teaching I've ever had on that. And I think that's biblically sound. There's no condemnation.
> *(beat)*

But you're celibate.

DAVID: I think what I saw in the church was far more listening to pressure groups and the kind of flavour of the century. Or the month. Than really coming to grips with historical faith and some of those things that are contained, I would say, in the biblical . . .

                    (pause)

Understanding.

The priest *who took over St. Alban's: Confident, articulate and serious, but quick to smile–30s. He was wearing a clerical collar. Interviewed in Denny's. We ate breakfast and he sipped coffee.*

THE NEW PRIEST: From homosexuality and ordination and blessing same sex unions, ordination of women—a lot of our issues do come down to how is scripture viewed, and usd, and authority. But even those who say that the scripture is to be taken literally still disagree on their interpretation of literal scripture so it's . . . it can turn around and bite you on your rear end—
(laughs)

No matter where you stand on it . . .

This would be my example . . .

Take the issue of Jubilee. Are we willing as a society to say every fiftieth year that all debts are forgiven—financial and otherwise?

And this is my problem with it.

If we're going to use scripture to say that homosexuality is an abomination before the Lord, will we also stone all those caught in the act of homosexuality?
(beat)

That's in the Bible. Children who don't obey their parents—will we kill them, as we're given permission in the Bible . . . There are things that we won't do as a society and yet it flies in the face of what the scripture says we should do . . . Based on what? Some have come around to say that . . . issues of cleanliness and . . . food are . . .

were cultural things for a specific time and they're not moral issues that we have to follow today as a code. That was a huge issue for the people of Paul's time. In his writings there were those who felt very strongly you could never eat anything sacrificed to idols. That that was wrong. If you ate meat that had been sacrificed from an animal, sacrificed to an idol, that that was sinful. And he said, for those of you who feel that way, that's your interpretation of scripture and that's what keeps you in a relationship with God, go with it. Those of you who know that idols don't exist and it's just a piece of meat and you're hungry and you want to eat it and your relationship with God stays the same, eat it. But don't make one of the other group have that become a stumbling block for their faith.
(two beats)

Will we ever be able to reach that understanding about homosexuality? That it becomes . . .

An issue of interpretation, an issue of culture, an issue of . . .seeing the world differently from what it was seen three thousand or four thousand years ago?

I don't know.

This may be something that we eventually overcome as we have revision of hymn books and ordination of women. And it may be something that causes another . . . another branch of Anglicanism. In a way it's happened here . . . in terms of . . .

From what I understand, Alberni Christian Fellowship is still using the Book of Alternative Services as its form of worship. So there was an aspect of that that they wanted to keep. There's another group within the Anglican church. Can't remember the exact name of them . . .

It's the Anglo-Catholic Church or the Catholic-Anglican Church. Something like that. That one of their issues was the ordination of women and so they left and formed their own version of the Anglican Church and they're very Anglo-Catholic in their theology and their worship, their liturgy . . . It has happened . . . England, three or five years ago, said if the Queen allows the ordination of women we'll leave the Church in droves and go to the Church of Rome. Women are ordained in England now and very few people went . . .

Sometimes it's sort of the last threat that somebody can give. But will they do it?

REPORTER: *Diocesan Post*, January 1999—Calgary congregation forms own Church. *Diocesan Post*, March 2000—Congregation in Houston leaves . . . *Globe and Mail*, March 17, 2000—Churches threaten to split over Same Sex blessing.

David *&* The Vancouver Island Priest *both take focus.*

DAVID: One of the things that I have been most angered and hurt by is this continual rhetoric . . .

I can love you as a person and disagree with your lifestyle. As you can to me. And I fundamentally cannot make the jump of saying I believe that homosexual lifestyle is as natural—it can be natural in a relative way—but as ordained by God maybe I should say, for want of better words . . . I don't think it's on the same level as marriage. Heterosexual marriage.

VANCOUVER ISLAND PRIEST: One of his favourite lines always was—I'm not homophobic, I'm just against homosexuals having sex.
(laughs for a few seconds, then stops)

In my coming out speech at the clergy conference I said, "We hear all this stuff about homosexual acts and refraining from homosexual acts." And I said, "Well, as far as I'm concerned, for me, breathing is a homosexual act. And to ask me to refrain from it is asking me . . .

Is asking me to die."

YOUTH PASTOR: The Anglican church is doomed to repeat St. Alban's because they don't see it as St. Alban's, they see it as David . . . They're doomed to repeat it. The writing's on the wall. Because they're not willing to see it as something that's morally consistent with the whole church and not just one person.

Youth Pastor *begins to sing the opening hymn. Then the other actors join him in the hymn from the opening. And, finally, they're joined by the* Vancouver Island Priest and David.

CURTAIN

ACT II

The purpose of this play is to spark discussion.

The hope is that it will provide an opportunity for individuals—and congregations—to discuss the blessing of same sex unions.

This act belongs to you and so, ultimately, does the ending.

Biographical Note

Mark Leiren-Young is a Canadian playwright, screenwriter and journalist. As a playwright he's best known for his controversial dramas (including *Shylock, Basically Good Kids and Dim Sum Diaries*) and political and social satires (including dozens of topical revues with his comedy duo, Local Anxiety). Mark's plays have been produced at theatres across Canada and have also been seen in the U.S. and Australia. Mark's television writing credits include episodes of *Captain Lightning, Toy Castle, Mentors, Psi Factor, Jonovision, Stickin' Around, ReBoot, Grand Illusions*, CBC's *Life and Times* and the award-winning TV special, *Greenpieces—An Eco-Comedy*, which he also co-produced and co-starred in. As a journalist, Mark has written for *Time, Maclean's, The Utne Reader* and dozens of other newspapers and magazines. He is co-author of *The Little Book of Reform* and has released one CD with Local Anxiety, *Forgive Us, We're Canadian*. For more information about Mark, and any of his plays, visit www.leiren-young.ca.

    Other plays by the author:
        Shylock (also published by Anvil Press)
        Blueprints from Space
        Basically Good Kids
        If You Really Love Me . . .
        Dim Sum Diaries
        Easy Money (music by Bruce Kellett)
        Greenpieces (music by Kevin Crofton)
        Jim
        Watchin'